LAKE CLASSICS

*Great American
Short Stories III*

Theodore
DREISER

Stories retold by Prescott Hill
Illustrated by James Balkovek

LAKE EDUCATION
Belmont, California

LAKE CLASSICS

Great American Short Stories I

Washington Irving, Nathaniel Hawthorne, Mark Twain, Bret Harte, Edgar Allan Poe, Kate Chopin, Willa Cather, Sarah Orne Jewett, Sherwood Anderson, Charles W. Chesnutt

Great American Short Stories II

Herman Melville, Stephen Crane, Ambrose Bierce, Jack London, Edith Wharton, Charlotte Perkins Gilman, Frank R. Stockton, Hamlin Garland, O. Henry, Richard Harding Davis

Great American Short Stories III

Thomas Bailey Aldrich, Irvin S. Cobb, Rebecca Harding Davis, Theodore Dreiser, Alice Dunbar-Nelson, Edna Ferber, Mary Wilkins Freeman, Henry James, Ring Lardner, Wilbur Daniel Steele

Great British and Irish Short Stories

Arthur Conan Doyle, Saki (H. H. Munro), Rudyard Kipling, Katherine Mansfield, Thomas Hardy, E. M. Forster, Robert Louis Stevenson, H. G. Wells, John Galsworthy, James Joyce

Great Short Stories from Around the World

Guy de Maupassant, Anton Chekhov, Leo Tolstoy, Selma Lagerlöf, Alphonse Daudet, Mori Ogwai, Leopoldo Alas, Rabindranath Tagore, Fyodor Dostoevsky, Honoré de Balzac

Cover and Text Designer: Diann Abbott

Library of Congress Catalog Number: 95-76748
ISBN 1-56103-066-X
Printed in the United States of America
1 9 8 7 6 5 4 3 2 1

CONTENTS

❦ Lake Classic Short Stories ❦

"The universe is made of stories, not atoms."
    —Muriel Rukeyser

"The story's about you."
    —Horace

Everyone loves a good story. It is hard to think of a friendlier introduction to classic literature. For one thing, short stories are *short*—quick to get into and easy to finish. Of all the literary forms, the short story is the least intimidating and the most approachable.

Great literature is an important part of our human heritage. In the belief that this heritage belongs to everyone, *Lake Classic Short Stories* are adapted for today's readers. Lengthy sentences and paragraphs are shortened. Archaic words are replaced. Modern punctuation and spellings are used. Many of the longer stories are abridged. In all the stories, painstaking care has been taken to preserve the author's unique voice.

Lake Classic Short Stories have something for everyone. The hundreds of stories in the collection cover a broad terrain of themes, story types, and styles. Literary merit was a deciding factor in story selection. But no story was included unless it was as enjoyable as it was instructive. And special priority was given to stories that shine light on the human condition.

Each book in the *Lake Classic Short Stories* is devoted to the work of a single author. Little-known stories of merit are included with famous old favorites. Taken as a whole, the collected authors and stories make up a rich and diverse sampler of the story-teller's art.

Lake Classic Short Stories guarantee a great reading experience. Readers who look for common interests, concerns, and experiences are sure to find them. Readers who bring their own gifts of perception and appreciation to the stories will be doubly rewarded.

❧ Theodore Dreiser ❧
(1871–1945)

About the Author

Born in Terre Haute, Indiana, Theodore Dreiser was the son of an extremely religious father and a sensitive, caring mother. The Dreiser family was very poor. At an early age, Theodore was ready to escape from poverty and his father's harsh ideas of religion.

After a year at the University of Indiana, Dreiser went to work as a newspaper reporter. In the next few years he wrote for papers in Chicago, St. Louis, Pittsburgh, and New York.

In 1900, Dreiser's first (and some say his greatest) novel, *Sister Carrie*, was accepted for publication. Before any copies went on the market, however, the publisher withdrew the book. There were complaints that it was too frank and that it ignored the morals of the day.

At first, Dreiser was depressed. Then he got angry—angry enough to begin a fight against censorship. For the rest of his days, he battled for the right of an author to present life as he sees it.

In 1927, Dreiser visited Russia. After his return, his writing became more concerned with socialism and politics.

Dreiser was a big, slow-moving man. He had a large, powerful forehead and, in his own words, "a lumpy chin." He was once described as having "strangely blazing steel-gray eyes." They were the eyes of a man who never gave in to pressures. In his entire career, he never compromised his writing or his beliefs. Theodore Dreiser wrote what he chose without worrying about public opinion.

The
Lost Phoebe

Are some heartaches too great to bear? In this famous story of loss and love, an ordinary old man goes to extraordinary lengths to find his lost mate.

"WHY, YOUR WIFE AIN'T HERE, HENRY. BUT YOU COME IN AND SIT DOWN."

The Lost Phoebe

The two of them lived together in the country, about three miles outside of town. The population of the town was small and getting smaller. More people were leaving it than coming in. The few farms around grew mostly corn and wheat. Their nearest neighbor lived about a mile away.

Their house was part log and part frame. The log part had belonged to Henry's grandfather. The newer frame part was not really new. Henry had built it when he was 21 years old and just married. That was 48 years ago.

The furniture inside the house was old, too. There was an old-fashioned four-poster bed. The chest of drawers was old-fashioned as well.

The living room carpet was a faded, gray and pink thing. Phoebe Ann had made it herself 15 years before she died. The loom she wove it on was still in a side room. Now it stood like a dusty, wooden skeleton. Next to it was a broken rocking chair. Next to that was a worn-down bench—heaven knows how old.

Broken-down furniture was scattered throughout the house. There was a sewing machine that no longer worked. There was an old, cracked mirror. The day their youngest son died it had fallen from the wall.

The orchard to the east of the house was full of old apple trees. The trunks and branches were worm-eaten. There were also several broken-down out-buildings near the house. One had been a chicken coop. Another had been a barn for horses and cows. There was a tumble-down shed where pigs had been kept. The roofs of those buildings were falling in. The sides were bleached by the sun. It was hard to believe they had once been painted.

The picket fence in front was falling apart. The side fences were rundown, too. They had aged right along with the old couple who lived here—a Mr. Henry Reifsneider and his wife, Phoebe Ann.

The two of them had lived here since their marriage 48 years before. Henry had lived here since his childhood. His parents had died ten years after he and Phoebe were married. After that Henry and Phoebe shared the house with their own children.

Of the seven children born to them, three had died. One girl had gone to Kansas. One boy had gone to Sioux Falls, never to be heard from again. Another boy had gone to Washington. The last girl lived five counties away.

None of their children gave much thought to the old couple.

Old Henry Reifsneider and his wife Phoebe were a loving couple. Maybe you know how it is with simple people. The great world has no call for them. They have no great thoughts. They are happy enough with the orchard, the meadow, the cornfield, the pig pen. Beyond these things, there is little else.

Old Henry and his wife Phoebe were very fond of each other. There was not much else in their lives to be fond of. He was a thin old man of 70 when she died. The hair on his head was wispy and gray. So was his beard, a straggly thing. Henry's eyes were dull, fishy, and watery. They had deep crow's feet at the sides. His clothes were old and baggy, worn out at the elbows and knees. Phoebe Ann was thin and shapeless, too. She always dressed in black. Even her best bonnet was black.

As time had passed, their activities had become fewer and fewer. They only kept one pig and a single horse. Most of their chickens were gone. Some were eaten by foxes. Others died from lack of care. The once healthy garden was now just a memory.

Henry and Phoebe had made a will. It divided the property among their remaining four children. But the place was small, and there were too many taxes owed on it. The children had no real interest in the old place.

Yet these two people lived together in peace and sympathy. Oh, now and then Henry would become cranky. He'd complain about little things that were of no importance.

"Phoebe, where's my corn knife? You never leave my things alone."

"Now you hush, Henry," his wife would reply. "If you don't, I'll leave you. I'll get up and walk out of here someday. Then where would you be? You ain't got nobody but me to look after you. So you just behave yourself. Your corn knife is on the mantel where you always put it."

Old Henry knew his wife would never leave him. But he used to wonder what he would do if she died. That was the only thing that he really feared.

Sometimes, as he wound the big clock at night, he'd think about that. It was a comfort to know that Phoebe was in bed. If he woke up during the night, she would be there beside him.

"Now, Henry, do lie still!" she would say. "You're as restless as a chicken."

"But I can't sleep, Phoebe."

"Well, you don't have to roll around, do you? You can let *me* sleep."

This usually relaxed him.

He liked doing things for her. If she wanted a pail of water, he might complain out of habit. But he'd get it with pleasure. Sometimes she got up first and built the fire. So he always made sure the wood for it was cut. In these little ways, they divided their simple world nicely between them.

As the years had passed, fewer and fewer people came by. The two of them were well-known in the area as old Mr. and Mrs. Reifsneider. People thought they were decent folks, but they were too old to be interesting.

They rarely wrote letters. And they rarely got any. Now and then old friends might stop by. The friends might bring a pie or cake or roasted chicken. But that didn't happen often.

Then one day in the spring of her 64th year, Mrs. Reifsneider took sick. It started out as just a low fever. Soon, however, it became serious. Old Henry drove to Swinnerton, the next town, and got a doctor. Some friends came over to help, and the care for her was taken off Henry's hands.

Then one chilly spring night, she died. Old Henry was lost in a fog of sorrow. Friends invited him to stay with them. But he didn't accept. Henry was old and fixed in his ideas. He was used to the place he had known all his days. He could not think of leaving. He wanted to remain near Phoebe's grave.

The fact that he would have to live alone did not seem to trouble him. His children offered to take care of him, but he refused.

"I can take care of myself," he told everyone. "I can cook a little. Besides, it don't take much more than coffee and bread in the morning to satisfy me. I'll get along well enough. Just let me be."

Finally people took him at his word. They left him to himself.

For a while he sat around in the spring sun, just thinking. He tried to get interested in farming again. But he couldn't. When he came in from the fields, there was no Phoebe to meet him. It didn't feel right.

It was worse because so many of her things were around. Little by little, Henry put a few of her things away. At night he sat beside his lamp and read. Sometimes he read the newspaper. He also started reading the Bible, which he had neglected for years.

But mostly he looked at the floor as he sat there. He would think of what had become of Phoebe. He also thought about how soon he himself would die. Every day he made his coffee and ate some bread in the morning. At night he might fry himself a little bacon. But mostly his appetite was gone.

For five long months Henry lived this sad life. Then a change began.

It started one night, after he'd gone to bed. He could see the moon through the east windows. It threw shadows on the wooden floor. It made the old furniture stand out dimly in the room. As usual, he was thinking of how much he missed Phoebe. By midnight he was asleep. But he awoke at two.

By this time the moon had moved. It threw shadows from a different angle. One of the shadows made a strange pattern. It was the figure of a person leaning over a table. It looked just like Phoebe when she did the same thing! The sight gave him a great start. Could it really be she—or her ghost? He had never believed in spirits, but still . . .

Henry looked hard at the figure in the dim light. The figure did not move. He put his thin legs out of the bed and sat up. He and Phoebe had sometimes talked of ghosts. But they had never agreed that such things could be. She never believed her spirit could return to walk the earth. Yet here she was now. He could see her bending over the table. She seemed to be wearing her familiar black skirt.

"Phoebe!" he called. He stuck out his bony hand. "Have you come back?"

The figure did not move, so he got up and walked to the door. Then the shadowy form disappeared. All he could see was his coat over the chair, the lamp by the paper, and the half-open door.

"Well," he said to himself, "I thought *sure* I saw her." He ran his hand through his hair and shook his head. It must have been just a shadow. But seeing that dim figure gave him the idea that she might return.

A few nights later he looked out the window by his bed. A faint mist rose from the damp ground. In that mist, he thought he saw her again. The mist rose right where she used to stand when she fed the chickens.

He sat up and watched it closely. Could it be Phoebe? Had she returned to comfort him in his loneliness? What other way would she have? How else could she show herself? He stared hard at the low cloud of mist until a slight breath of air blew it away.

A third night, he dreamed she came to his bedside. Henry could feel her put her hand on his head.

"Poor Henry!" she said. "It's too bad."

He woke up and thought he saw her. She seemed to move from his bedroom into the living room. Her figure was a shadowy mass of black.

He got out of bed, convinced that Phoebe was coming back to him—if he only thought about her enough. If he made it clear that he needed her, she would come back! She had been such a kind wife. He knew she would try to come back and make him less lonely.

Night after night Henry waited, expecting her return. Once he thought he saw a pale light moving about the room. Another time, after dark, he thought he saw his dead wife walking in the orchard.

Then one morning he decided that she was not dead. Just *why* he believed that is hard to say. The thing was, his mind had gone. In its place was a dream, a kind of fixed illusion.

Didn't she used to say that she might leave him? It was always in a joking way, of course.

"I guess I could find you again," he had always told her.

Then she'd say, "You won't find me if I ever leave you. I guess I can get some place where you can't find me."

When he got up that morning, he did not make coffee. He was much too busy thinking about where to search for Phoebe. After he was dressed, he took his cane from behind the door. Then he headed for his nearest neighbor's house. His old shoes clumped in the dust as he walked. His gray hair was quite long now. It looked something like a halo.

Farmer Dodge met him on the road. "Why, hello, Henry!" he said. "Where are you going so early?" He hadn't seen Henry since the old man's wife had died. Farmer Dodge was surprised to see him looking so cheerful.

"You ain't seen Phoebe, have you?" Henry asked his neighbor.

"Phoebe who?" said Farmer Dodge. For the moment he didn't connect the name with Henry's dead wife.

"Why, my *wife* Phoebe, of course," Henry said. "Who do you think I mean?" He frowned at Farmer Dodge from under his shaggy gray eyebrows.

"Well, I'll be! You ain't joking, are you?" said Dodge. "It can't be your wife you're talking about. She's dead."

"*Dead!* Shucks!" said Henry. "She left early this morning, while I was sleeping. We had a little spat last night. That must be the reason. But I guess I can find her. I bet she's gone over to Matilda Race's."

Henry started walking briskly up the road. The amazed Farmer Dodge stared in wonder after him.

"Well, I'll be switched!" he muttered to himself. "He's clean out of his head. That poor old man has lost his mind. I'll have to tell the doctor to come out and take a look at him."

It was three miles to Jack and Matilda Race's place. Henry met no one else on the way. He passed several other houses, but didn't stop. When he got to the Race house, he knocked on the door.

"Why, hello, Mr. Reifsneider," said old Matilda Race. "What brings you here this morning?"

"Is Phoebe here?" he asked eagerly.

"Phoebe who? What Phoebe?" replied Mrs. Race.

"Why, *my* Phoebe, of course. My *wife* Phoebe. Who do you suppose? Ain't she here now?"

"My goodness!" said Mrs. Race. "You poor man! You come right in and sit down. Let me get you a cup of coffee. I'm sorry, but your wife ain't here. But you come and sit down. I'll find her for you, after a while. I know where she is."

The old farmer's eyes softened, and he entered the house.

Mrs. Race felt so sorry for him. He was so thin and pale. And she saw right away that he had lost his mind.

"We had a quarrel last night. I guess she left me," Henry said.

"Dear, dear!" said Mrs. Race aloud. But to herself she said, "The poor man! Now somebody's just got to look after him. He can't be allowed to run around the country looking for his dead wife. It's terrible."

She made him coffee and brought him some bread and butter. She set out some of her best jam with it.

"Now you stay right there," she said. "When Jack comes in, I'll send him to look for Phoebe. I think she's over in town with some of her friends. Anyhow, we'll find out. Now you just drink this coffee and eat this bread. You must be mighty tired. You've had a long walk this morning."

When her husband came home, Matilda would tell him about Henry. Then Jack could tell the Reifsneider children to come look after him.

Henry paid no attention to Matilda. He was thinking about his wife. Maybe she was visiting the Murray family. They lived miles and miles away in another direction. Suddenly he decided he wouldn't wait for Jack Race to hunt for Phoebe. He'd find her himself.

"Well, I'll be going now," he said to Matilda. He looked around blankly. "I guess she didn't come here after all. She must have gone over to the Murrays'. I won't wait any longer. There's a lot to do over at the house today."

Then he marched out in spite of her protests. He took to the dusty road again, his cane pounding the earth as he went.

Two hours later he appeared in the Murrays' doorway. He had walked five miles and it was now noon. An amazed husband and wife listened sadly to his strange story. They also realized that he was mad.

The Murrays begged Henry to stay for lunch. Later, they planned to tell the authorities and see what could be done.

Henry ate a little, but he didn't stay for long. In an hour or so, he was off again to another distant farmhouse.

So it went for that day and the next and the next. Henry roamed all over the countryside. Almost everyone agreed that he had lost his mind. But they also agreed that he was harmless.

The authorities were informed—the local county sheriff, no less. He, too, considered Henry harmless. His wandering around hurt no one. It was decided to let him remain at large. After all, he returned home every night. Why should they lock up an old man who bothered no one?

Many people were willing to do what they could for Henry. They gave him food, old clothes, the odds and ends of daily life. Soon everyone got used to him.

They were always quick to answer his question. "Why, no, Henry, I ain't seen her," they'd say. Or, "No, Henry, she ain't been here today."

He'd thank them and then be on his way.

Month after month, he went on in the same way. The odd old figure walked in sunshine and in rain, on dusty roads and muddy ones. But then his health grew frail. The longer he roamed, the deeper became his strange belief. He began to wander farther and farther from home. Finally he began taking a few utensils

with him from his house. That way he
didn't have to return home each night.
He carried a coffee pot, a plate, a cup,
knife, fork, and spoon. Along the way,
people gave him what little food he
wanted.

Henry's hair grew longer and longer.
His once tan hat turned dark brown with
dirt. His clothes grew thin and worn. For
several years Henry walked about this
way. Sometimes he slept in people's
barns. Sometimes he found shelter in
caves and under trees.

At first he had looked for Phoebe only
at people's houses. But then he began to
call for her in the woods and fields. Many
a farmer or hunter heard his cry. "O-o-o
Phoebe! O-o-o Phoebe!"

Whenever they heard it, they would
say, "There goes old Henry Reifsneider.
What a shame!"

Sometimes Henry puzzled about which
way to wander. Finally he came up with
an idea. He decided that Phoebe's spirit
would help him if he did the following:
First, he had to close his eyes and spin

around three times. Then he had to call out, "O-o-o Phoebe!" twice. Finally, he had to throw his cane in the air. When it landed, he would see which way it was pointing. Then he would go in that direction. Sometimes the cane would point the way he had just come from. Then he'd shake his head sadly. But off he'd go in that direction.

In the middle of the day sometimes his feet would get sore, and his legs would feel tired. Then he would stop to rest for a while. Soon, though, he would be up again.

Finally, Henry's strange figure came to be known in three or four counties. Old Reifsneider became a famous figure of sorrow.

* * *

Near a little town called Watersville was a place called Red Cliff. It was nothing more than a steep wall of red sandstone, about 100 feet high. The cliff could be seen for miles around. On the top was a thick grove of trees. A road led up to it on the other side.

In fair weather it was one of Henry's favorite places. He'd fry his bacon or boil his eggs at the foot of some tree. Then he'd make his bed under the trees.

Sometimes Henry would wake up in the night and start walking. He would stop at lonely road crossings and call out for Phoebe. When no answer came, he'd keep going.

One night in his seventh year of wandering, Henry came to Red Cliff. His cane had led him there. Henry had walked many miles that day. It was after ten o'clock at night when he reached the grove. He was so tired he could hardly stand. He set himself down in the dark to rest, and possibly to sleep.

For some reason, though, he felt that Phoebe was near. It would not be long now, he thought. Soon he would be seeing her again. After a time, he fell asleep with his head on his knees. At midnight the moon began to rise. When he awoke at two o'clock in the morning, the moon was high in the night sky.

The feeling that Phoebe was near grew stronger. He stared into the night. What was that moving in the distant shadows along the path? Was it moonlight and shadows? Was it mist, lighted by the moon? Was it fireflies?

Could it be his lost Phoebe?

Henry imagined that he could see her eyes. She was not as she was when he last saw her. Now she was a younger Phoebe. She was the happy, sweet Phoebe he had known many years before, when she was a girl.

Old Henry Reifsneider got up from the cold ground. All these years he had been waiting for this hour! Suddenly he could see her. There was her sweet smile. There was her soft brown hair. There was the light blue sash she had worn to a church picnic years ago.

Henry walked around the base of the tree, following eagerly after the slender young figure.

"Oh, Phoebe! Phoebe!" he called. "Have you really come to me? Have you really answered me?"

On and on he hurried after the light. He brushed against the trees, scratching his hands and face against twigs. His hat was gone. His lungs were breathless.

He came to the edge of the cliff and looked down. Then he saw her below— among a silvery bed of apple trees.

"Oh, Phoebe!" he called. "Wait, Phoebe! Oh, no, don't leave me!"

Suddenly, he remembered a world where love was young. A world where he and Phoebe were young. He gave out a great cry of joy, "Oh, wait, Phoebe!" And he leaped.

A few days later some farm boys found Henry's utensils. He'd left them under the tree. They found his old hat hanging on a bush. Then they found his body at the foot of the cliff. There was a peaceful smile on his face.

No one ever knew his joy in finding his lost mate.

The Cruise
of the Idlewild

A bit of fantasy can help to
pass the time and lighten
the heart. Why did little Ike
get tired of pretending?
Read on to find out.

"THE BOYS ON THEM BIG FANCY BOATS KNOW HOW TO
LIVE! WOULDN'T THAT BE A PERFECT LIFE FOR ME?"

The Cruise
of the Idlewild

It is hard to say now just how the trouble began. Of course, it is also hard to say how we ever managed to sail the *Idlewild* in the first place. But that is what this story is all about.

Some of us were pretty tired of the life we were leading. We all worked together, making furniture at a shop. But the work had become old and boring.

We had about 100 men in the shop. There were blacksmiths, carpenters, and painters there. We also had an engineer and a foreman. The foreman was in charge of all the workers.

Three or four of us used to get together to relax in the engine room. John, the engineer, was one of us. He ran the steam engine that powered the shop. He was sort of a big round fellow.

The blacksmith was also there. He was a small, wiry man, about 35 years old. His face always showed good humor. We called him the "village smith."

Then there was little Ike, the blacksmith's helper. He was as strange a cabin boy as ever served on an ocean-going steamer—or in a blacksmith's shop. Ike's face was always dirty. His pants were about four times too large for him. Where he got them was a mystery. He had big yellow teeth, with two or three missing. His eyes were small, and his hands were large. But all in all, he was a sweet soul. Poor little Ike! To think he was almost driven from his job by our foolishness!

I should say here that the *Idlewild* was not a boat at all. It was an *idea*.

The idea came up because our shop was near the water. It was located on

Long's Point, where the Harlem River meets the Hudson River. There was water to the south of us, water to the west, and water to the north. Behind us was a railroad yard.

Anyhow, our shop seemed a lot like a boat, what with all that water around us. We decided we'd call it the *Idlewild*. The men made up the crew, and the engineer was the captain. I was the mate. We pretended it was a real ship.

As I said, I don't know exactly how the idea started. Old John was always admiring the yachts that passed by on the Hudson River. Maybe that gave us the idea. Old John didn't really know all that much about boats. Still, he loved to talk about them.

"That must be Morgan's yacht," he said one day, pointing. "And there's the *Waterfowl*, Governor Morton's yacht. Wouldn't I like to sit on her deck and smoke big dollar cigars!" Then he laughed, "Aw, haw!"

"Right-o," I said.

"Aw, haw! The boys on all them big

fancy boats, they know how to live! Come now—wouldn't that be perfect for me?"

"It truly would," I replied. Then I decided to tease him. "Only I don't think you're doing so badly as it is. I notice you're not losing any flesh."

"I'm a little plump, I'll admit," he said. "I ain't as active as I used to be. A yacht, a dollar cigar, and a cool breeze would do for me."

"Well, John, I believe you're quite right," I said. "But you better get busy. It's time to shovel some wood shavings into the oven now. Just while you're waiting for your yacht and all. I notice your steam is getting low."

"Hang the steam!" he said. "If the company was decent they'd give us coal to burn instead of wood chips! It takes a hundred tons of shavings a day to keep this old engine going. All I do here is shovel. I'm an engineer, not a fireman. They ought to give me a helper."

"Quite so! Quite so!" I said. "But for now, back to the shovel, John!"

* * *

Out of such fooling around came the spirit of the *Idlewild*.

One day I said, "Why don't we have a boat of our own, John? We're almost in the water anyway. This shop is as good as any boat. We can call her the *Idlewild*. The men will provide the 'idle' part. The bosses will provide the 'wild.' How's that for a name—the *Idlewild*?"

"Haw! Haw!" said John. "Good idea! We'll fix her up today. You be the captain and I'll be the mate and—"

"No, no, John," I said. From his engine room he had the best view of the water. It was almost like a captain's cabin on a ship. "*You* be the captain, and *I'll* be the mate. This is a plenty good enough cabin. I'm satisfied to be the mate. Now open up steam, Captain, and we'll be off. Look out the window and see how she blows. 'It's ho! for a life on the bounding main, and a jolly old crew are we!'"

"Right-o, my hearty!" he said. He slapped me on the back. Then he reached for a lever on the engine and let off a blast of steam. With that the whistle blew, and we pretended the *Idlewild* was on the move.

The idea that we were aboard a real yacht delighted me. I could tell that it delighted John, too. Clearly, we needed some such dream. Outside was the blue water of the river. Far up and down were many fine sailing crafts like ours, I said to myself.

Inside of 15 minutes we had given out titles. The blacksmith was the bosun. Little Ike—the smith's helper—was the bosun's mate. The other workers made up the rest of the crew. In our minds, the engine room was now the captain's cabin. It was filled with sailor talk. You could hear shouts of, "Heave ho!" "Shiver my timbers!" and so on. We thought we sounded like real men of the sea.

We "heaved ho" at seven in the morning when the engine started. When it stopped at noon, we "dropped anchor."

On hot days we pretended to sail to Coney Island or Newport. Since it was all pretend, we could go anywhere! Many times we visited Paris, London, and Rome. We'd do it all in the same hour. But we were always back where we started by quitting time.

During the days that followed, we built on our idea. The *Idlewild* began to seem *real*. If you've never played such a game, that might be a bit hard for you to understand. But for us, our shop had become a ship. The ship's wheel was at the stern—where the carpenters worked. The anchor was at the bow—where the steam engine was.

There was a new light in the captain's eye. I think he sometimes really believed he was on a ship. It's easy to believe such things when it's fun to do so. And it was such a relief from the actual work we did! It sure beat carrying shavings. That was my job. No wonder I valued my title of mate on a yacht.

Little Ike was a bit slow. At first he didn't quite get the meaning of our game. But at last it dawned on him. When he finally got the idea, he was very pleased.

"Gee!" he said, "*me*, a bosun's mate! That's the real thing, ain't it!"

"But remember, this is the *captain's* cabin," I said. "The bosun's mate has to be respectful. You have to obey the captain's orders. If he wants you to shovel shavings, you'd better do it."

"Not on your life," Ike replied. He understood well enough that this meant more work for him.

"That's right, though," John said to Ike. He was very pleased with my latest idea. "*I'm* the captain here. You don't want to forget that. No back talk from any bosun's mate. And what the mate says goes, too."

Then John smiled. "Why don't you shovel some shavings now?" he added.

"No! I will not!" said Ike.

"Come on now, Ike," I said. "You can't go back on the captain now. We have leg irons for people who won't obey."

I eyed a pile of rusty old chains lying outside the door. "We might have to chain him up, Captain," I said with a wink. I picked up the chain and rattled it.

The captain half choked with laughter when he saw what I was doing.

"That's right," he said. "Go get the shovel there, Ike."

Ike didn't like the idea very much. But he went along with it. After eight shovelfuls we told him that was enough. The captain and I were pleased that Ike had obeyed orders. It set a good example.

After that, things went from good to even better. We brought a carpenter's helper named Joe into our game. We told him he could have the job of "day watch." That meant he was to look for "suspicious lights" at sea. If he saw anything he was to come and report to us. That fit in with his real job. He was always walking back and forth in the shop, carrying boards.

Good old Joe! I can see him now. He was tall and a little bent over. His head bobbed like a duck's when he walked. He was a most agreeable person. His dreams were so simple, his wants so few. He was paid only 20 cents an hour. He deserved much more. Maybe our game added something to his life, too.

"Light on the starboard bow." That was the way we had him report. Or "Light on the port bow." And we insisted he call us "Sir." That was to show proper respect.

When Joe would leave, the captain always said, "I think our crew is working out well."

"Oh, yes, I think we've got them going, Captain," I'd say.

"Nothing like order."

"You're right, Captain."

"I don't suppose the mate would take orders like that," John would say.

"Well, hardly, Captain," I'd answer.

"Still, you don't want to forget that *I'm* the captain, Mate."

"And you don't want to forget that *I'm* the mate, Captain."

Lots of times we would joke back and forth like that.

Things then went from better to best. After a while, most of the men in the shop were playing the game. There were some exceptions, though—the foreman, for one. The foreman was not much for pretending. He thought our game was foolish. He thought it got in the way of our work. His red hair, big hands, and big feet made him look like a scarecrow. And he was deadly dull. He had no imagination at all beyond lumber and furniture. The man simply had no poetry in his soul.

The rest of the workers accepted the game as a relief from boredom. They wanted to think they were not really working in a dirty shop. They liked to pretend they were out on the blue sea.

"So, you're the captain, eh?" lazy old Jack the carpenter asked John one day.

"That I am, Jack," John replied. "But able seamen ain't supposed to ask too many questions." He looked toward me. "Ain't that right, Mate?"

"True," I said, arriving with a basket of shavings. "And able seamen should always salute the captain before speaking to him. And they should always call him 'Sir.' But then our crew is new. We expect a few mistakes now and then. Right, Captain?"

"Right, Mate," said John. "You're

always right—or nearly so, anyway."

Before I could start an argument on this matter, Stephen Bowers spoke up. He was one of the carpenters—and one of our able seamen.

"I don't know about you two being right," he said. "It seems to me the mate of this here ship ain't much. Nor the captain either."

' The captain and I were a little upset by this.

It seemed that Stephen was too dull to get the point of the game. And he was too big and strong for us to argue with. He was likely to take our jokes seriously. It threatened smooth sailing.

"Well, it looks like mutiny," I said.

"It *does* look that way, don't it?" big John said. He looked at Stephen with a little smile. "What will we do, Mate?"

"Lower a boat, Captain, and set him adrift," I suggested. "Or you could put him on bread and water, along with the foreman. He's the worst troublemaker aboard the boat."

"Oh, no, don't!" Stephen said, finally

getting the joke. "I don't want to be put in the same class as the foreman. I'm not *that* bad a person!"

"Very well, then," I replied. "What do you say, Captain?"

John looked at me and smiled. "Do you think we can let him go—just this once?"

"Sure," I replied. "If he's certain he doesn't want to join the foreman."

Old Bowers went away smiling.

We played the game all summer. It was fun—for almost everyone.

Unfortunately, we began to pick on little Ike a bit too much. He became the butt of a thousand jokes. The trouble was, he didn't really understand the jokes. But he was a gentle sort of person. He never complained. So we had our fun with him. We called upon him to shovel ashes. We had him split wood. We had him carry shavings. None of these tasks were part of his real job.

More than once we threatened to put Ike in chains. Once we actually started to wrap a chain around him. That caused a big struggle—almost a real fight.

Another time we had some fun with a big crate in the shop that a desk came in. We told him it was a jail, and we would put him in it.

Then we went too far.

This is what happened.

Ike had to clean the room where the blacksmith worked. He liked to sweep it up at three in the afternoon. If the floor got dirty after that, he'd get mad. But there were still three hours of work ahead of us. We didn't get off until six.

I had to carry shavings through there all this time. How could I help spilling a few? But I have to admit it. Sometimes I spilled them on purpose, just to tease Ike. After the captain and I talked it over, he gave Ike an order. From now on, Ike was to wait until five o'clock to sweep up.

Ike replied that the captain could "go to the devil." He said he wasn't going to kill himself for anybody. And besides, the foreman once told him he could do his sweeping at three.

Here was a stiff problem. Mutiny! Mutiny! Mutiny! What was to be done?

It was true we'd been picking on the bosun's mate. He was always doing a dozen things he didn't have to do. Still, if we were going to command the ship, we had to command *him*. At least that's what we thought at the time.

We decided to act. The next day Ike swept up at about three o'clock. As soon as he went to another part of the shop, we struck. We threw shavings all over his newly cleaned floor. It was great fun. We got a good laugh out of it—but it led to trouble.

Ike came back in and cleaned up the mess. He wasn't happy about it, though. He didn't take it as a joke. In fact he was very down about it. He called us names. He said he'd go to the foreman if we did it again.

Of course we did it again anyway. Not once, but several times after that. That was our mistake. At last, we'd pushed little Ike too far. He went to the foreman.

"I'm not going to stand for it," he told the foreman. "They're messing up my floor with shavings every time I clean it.

I'll quit if you don't make them stop."

The foreman—that terribly dull person—took Ike's side. He was tired of our game. He decided to stop it.

"I want you fellows to cut out this foolishness now," he told us. "Leave Ike alone. I've heard enough of this ship stuff. It's all nonsense."

The captain and I looked at each other without smiling. Could it be that Ike had turned traitor? This *was* mutiny! He had not only complained about us. He had complained about the ship itself—the wonderful *Idlewild*!

When the foreman left, John and I talked it over. What would we do? Would we let the ship sink, or try to save her? Perhaps we should drop the joke for a little while, at least as far as Ike was concerned. Little Ike might cause the whole ship to be destroyed.

We decided to say nothing to Ike. But we still had ways to punish him.

Ike loved the engine room. He often came there for a drink of water or to rest. He worked as hard as anyone—probably harder. But sometimes there were breaks in his work. The engine room was his favorite place to relax. At noon he could bring his cold coffee there to warm it up. There was a closet where he could hang his coat. There was a washtub with hot water for washing up. John had always allowed him to do these things.

Now this all changed. Why should he get away with mutiny? More as a joke than anything else, John told him the news. If he insisted on sweeping up at three o'clock, he couldn't come into the engine room anymore.

Then John turned to me and winked. "Well, Mate, what do you think?"

"You're right, Captain. Very right," I said. "You're on the right track now. No more favors—unless—"

"Oh, all right," replied little Ike. He didn't know we were joking. "If I can't, I can't. Just the same, I don't pick up no shavings after three." And off he walked.

Think of it. It was final and complete mutiny. And there was nothing more to be done. All that we could do was to see what would happen next.

When Ike had a break now, he really had no place to relax. And he had no one to talk to. The other men never much cared for him. He was a sad figure, with his funny clothes and big yellow teeth. The captain and the mate had been his only friends. And now they had deserted him. It was tough.

Then even more trouble came to the *Idlewild*. John and I began to argue about the ship. I thought I should have the most say in the game. After all, it had been my idea. He thought he should have the last say in things. After all, the center of activity was his engine room. Our argument began as a joke. But as the days passed, it got more serious. Without Ike around to tease, we began to get on each other's nerves. Before long we were barely on speaking terms.

Our crew saw that there was war in the captain's cabin. But they didn't want to take sides. It wasn't important enough in their hardworking lives.

And so—because the captain and mate

couldn't get along—the worst thing happened. The ship went down. Yes, she was lost. The *Idlewild* was gone. With her went all her fine seas, winds, distant cities, fogs, and storms.

For a long time after, John and I were careful. We couldn't be outright rude to each other. We still had to work in the same room. We had to find a way to work together. There had never been any real argument between us. It was just joking around. But it had gotten out of hand. And we both felt bad about it.

The problem was, how could we patch it up? We didn't have an answer for a long time. But little by little, we began to speak to each other. After a while, the quarrel was forgotten.

Then one day John said to me, "Remember the *Idlewild*, Henry?"

"That I do, Captain," I said to him pleasantly.

"Great old boat she was—wasn't she, Mate?"

"She surely was."

"And the bosun's mate—he wasn't so

bad, was he? Even if he wouldn't quit sweeping up the shavings."

"He certainly wasn't. He was a fine little fellow. Remember the chains?"

"Haw! Haw!" John laughed. "Do you think the old *Idlewild* could ever be found? I expect she's lying somewhere down on the bottom, Mate."

"Well, she might be, Captain. But she'd hardly be the same old boat. She's been down a long time. It might be easier to build a new one—don't you think?"

"I think you're right, Mate. What would we call her if we did?"

"Well, how about the *Harmony*, Captain? That should suit her."

"The *Harmony*, Mate? You're right— the *Harmony* is a fine name. Well, shall we do it? Put her there!"

"Put her there," I replied with a big smile. "We'll organize a new crew right away, Captain."

"Right! But, wait! Let's call the bosun and see what he says."

Just then the bosun appeared, smiling. "Well, what's up?" he asked. "You two ain't made up, have you?"

"We have, bosun," I said. "And what's more, we're thinking of raising the *Idlewild*. Or rather we're going to build a new boat—the *Harmony*."

"Well, I'm mighty glad to hear it. But I don't think you can have your old bosun's mate. He's going to quit."

"Going to *quit*!" we both cried out at the same moment.

John got serious then. "What's the trouble? Who's doing anything mean to him now?" We both felt guilty because of our part in his pains.

"Well, Ike kind of feels that the shop has been against him," said the bosun. "I don't really know why. He thinks you two have been trying to freeze him out. He says he can't do anything anymore. Says everybody makes fun of him and shuts him out."

Now we stared at each other, feeling ashamed. After all, we were plainly the cause of poor little Ike's feelings. And we were the only ones who could cheer him. It was the captain's cabin Ike was longing for—his old hangout.

"Oh, we can't lose Ike, Captain," I said. "What good would the *Harmony* be without him? We can't let anything like that happen, can we?"

"You're right, Mate," he replied. "There never was a better bosun's mate than Ike. The *Harmony*'s got to have him. Let's talk reason to him, if we can."

So we went to see him. And it wasn't to tease him. We wanted to plead with him not to leave the shop—or the ship. This time everything was going to be better than ever. We tried hard to convince him of that.

And we did.

McEwen of the Shining Slave Makers

McEwen only meant to take a rest in the shady park. The last thing he expected was to get caught up in a life and death adventure!

ONE ANT THAT WAS MORE ACTIVE THAN THE OTHERS
CAUGHT McEWEN'S EYE.

McEwen of the Shining Slave Makers

It was a hot day in August. The sun had faded the once-green leaves of the trees. Except in shady places, the grass was dry and brown. The roads were hot and thick with dust.

Robert McEwen sat under a beech tree. Its broad arms cast a welcome shade. He had come here to get away from the busy streets. He had come to relax.

He looked around the park. He wasn't thinking of anything special. Then he happened to notice an ant on his knee. He flipped it away with his finger.

Were there more ants on him? He stood

up and brushed himself off.

Then he noticed an ant running along in front of him. He stamped on it.

"I guess that will do for you," he said to himself. He sat down again.

Now McEwen looked closely at the walk. It was wide and hard and hot. *Many* ants were hurrying about there. He noticed how black they were. Finally, one ant more active than the others caught his eye.

The ant moved first to the right, then to the left. It stopped here and there, but never for more than a second. Its energy and movements interested McEwen.

As he stared, the path grew in his imagination. Soon it seemed to be huge.

He rubbed his eyes. Suddenly, he was walking in an unknown world! It was strange in every detail. The trees had disappeared. A forest of huge, flat, green swords swayed in the air above him. The ground underneath lacked a carpet of green. It was dry and covered with huge boulders of clay. Only the hot sun and the blue sky seemed familiar, and he himself felt a little bit strange.

McEwen's three pairs of limbs seemed natural enough. So did his mouth—his mandible, really. It was made up of two strong, biting jaws. The fact that he sensed, rather than saw things, seemed natural—and yet odd.

Suddenly he felt a sense of duty to hunt for food. It was as though he needed to find it for his tribe. He didn't quite know why, but he knew he must.

He walked along on his six feet until he came to a broad plain. It was so wide he couldn't see across it. He stopped and breathed deeply.

Just then he heard a voice behind him: "Anything to eat around here?"

McEwen turned. "I don't know," he said, "I have just—"

"This is terrible," cried the stranger, not waiting to hear his answer. "It looks like famine. You know the *Sanguineae* have gone to war."

"No," answered McEwen.

"Yes," said the other. "They raided the *Fuscae* yesterday. They'll be here next."

With that, the stranger took off.

The words *Sanguineae* and *Fuscae* did not seem strange to McEwen. Somehow he knew what the stranger was talking about. He didn't give the matter much thought. A strong hunger had come over him. He started after the stranger.

On the way he met another stranger. This one spoke to him, too. "I haven't found a thing today. I've been all the way to the *Pratensis* region. I didn't dare go farther. Not without some others coming with me. They're hungry, too, up there— though they've just made a raid. You heard the *Sanguineae* went to war?"

"Yes, he told me," said McEwen. He moved his head in the direction of the first stranger.

"Oh, you mean Ermi," the second one said. "Yes, he's been over in their territory. Well, I'll be going now."

McEwen hurried after Ermi. Before long he overtook him. Ermi had stopped. He had picked up a jagged crumb of food. It was almost as big as he was.

"Oh!" said McEwen eagerly, "where did

you get that big piece of food?"

"Here," said Ermi.

"Will you give me a little?" asked McEwen.

"I will *not*," said the other. An almost evil light shone in his eye.

"All right," said McEwen. "Which way would you advise me to look?"

"Wherever you please," said Ermi. "Why ask *me*? You're not new at seeking." Then he hurried away.

"The forest was better than this," McEwen thought. He was feeling hot. "I wouldn't die of the heat there, anyhow. And I might find food. Here there is nothing." He turned and glanced around, looking for the jungle he had come from.

Far to the left and behind him, he saw those huge green swords. As he looked that way, he saw another like himself hurrying toward him.

McEwen asked the new arrival a question. "Say, there! Do you know where I can get something to eat?"

The other one looked angry. "How can you ask such a thing in the time of great hunger? If I had anything for myself, I would not be out here. Go out and hunt for it, like the rest of us."

"But I *have* been hunting," cried out McEwen, his temper rising. "I've searched all around until I am almost starved."

"No worse off than any of us, are you?" said the other, meanly. "Look at *me*. Do you suppose I am feasting?" Then he hurried off in an angry huff.

McEwen looked after him until he was out of sight. Then he continued on his search. Soon he heard a weak voice. It sounded like someone in pain.

"Here—over here!" came the cry.

McEwen moved forward at once. When he was still a good distance away, he recognized the voice. The second stranger was lying on the ground. His mandibles were working slowly.

"What is it?" asked McEwen. "What ails you? How did this happen?"

"I don't know," said the other. "I was passing along here when *that* struck me." He nodded toward a huge boulder. "I am done for, though. You may as well have this food now. The tribe can use whatever you do not eat," he sighed.

"Oh, nothing of the sort," said McEwen. "You'll be all right. Why do you speak of death? Just tell me where to take you—or where to get help."

"No, it would be no use," said the other. "I didn't want help. There's nothing can be done for me. I just wanted you to have this food here. I won't be needing it now."

"Don't say that," said McEwen. "You mustn't talk about dying. There must be *something* I can do. Tell me! I don't want your food."

"No, there isn't anything you could do. There isn't any cure—you know that. When you return, tell the others how I was killed. And take that crumb along with you. The others need it, even if you do not."

McEwen looked at him silently. This talk of a tribe seemed to clear up many things for him. Now he remembered the long road that he had traveled. He remembered that the huge tribe lived

under the earth. There were passageways he had walked through many
times. There was the powerful and much-
loved ant mother. And there were the
eggs to be taken care of.

That was it! He was a *part* of this great
tribe. He knew that he must find food
for it. He must kill spiders, beetles,
grubs, and bring them back to the tribe.

Then the stranger gasped and died.

McEwen looked upon the body. He had
seen so many die that way. In times past,
he had reported the deaths of hundreds.

"Is he dead?" asked a voice at his side.
It was another stranger.

"Yes," said McEwen.

"Then he will not need this, I guess,"
said the other. And he picked up the huge
crumb with his mandibles.

But McEwen was alert. He, too,
snapped down hard upon the crumb.

"He said he wanted *me* to have this,"
McEwen shouted. "And I'm going to keep
it. Let go!"

"I will not," said the other with great
energy. "I'll have *some* of it, at least."

With that he gave a mighty pull, which sent both McEwen and himself to the ground. Then the stranger tore off a piece and took off quickly.

McEwen got up. He was too hungry to chase after the other. He ate as much of the crumb as he needed to satisfy his hunger. Then he rested for a bit.

After a time he headed off for the distant jungle. He felt sure that the tribe's home was in that direction. As he moved into the jungle, he heard the sound of marching feet. Not knowing what creatures he was about to meet, he hid behind a boulder.

Soon he saw them—a band of warriors. He knew who they were. They were slave makers like himself. But they were red. Somehow he knew they were the *Sanguineae* that Ermi had spoken of.

There was no doubt they were at war. Nearly every warrior carried some mark of plunder or of death. Many carried the dead bodies of the enemy in their mandibles. Others carried the heads of the blacks they'd killed.

McEwen stayed hidden until they were out of sight. He was about to come out when he saw something move near another boulder. It was Ermi, the one he had met before. He, too, had been hiding. Then Ermi began to run. Seconds later, four red warriors appeared. They had seen Ermi and were now chasing him.

McEwen hurried after them. As he got near, he saw Ermi. He was trying to block the entrance to a cave with a boulder.

The four *Sanguineae* were upon him, though. McEwen could see that they were cruel, murderous warriors. They were covered with battle scars. As they attacked, they shouted at each other.

One was called Og by the others. He had a scar on his head and the tip of his left antenna was broken. He tried to bite Ermi. Then Ermi fought back. With his mandibles, he grabbed the head of the red ant called Maru. Og went for Ermi's leg. Back and forth they all went, shouting loudly. At first, McEwen didn't want to get involved. But then he decided to come to his friend's rescue. Weren't they brothers of the same tribe?

McEwen leaped onto Og and grabbed his neck. He began to saw at it with his powerful teeth. That made Og let go of Ermi's leg and try to shake off his new enemy. But McEwen held on tight. Ponan and Om kept after Ermi, who had finally killed Maru.

Then Ponan grabbed Ermi's head.

"Kill him!" yelled Om. "Kill him!"

But this very moment, Og's head fell to the ground. McEwen rushed to Ermi's aid. He bit into Ponan's side and made him loosen his hold on Ermi. Now the fight was more desperate than ever. The warriors rolled and tossed around. McEwen's right antenna was broken and one of his legs was cut.

Ermi was a skilled fighter. He threw Om to the ground and left him stunned. Then he rushed to help McEwen. He hit Ponan from the side and knocked him down. In seconds, he and McEwen tore the *Sanguineae* warrior in two.

Om, meanwhile, was able to escape.

"Come with me," said Ermi to McEwen.

"Om will bring others. Come this way. Our home is in here." They went into the cave and closed it with stones.

"Stay with me," Ermi said. Leading the way, he took McEwen with him along secret passageways.

"You see how it is here," he said to McEwen. "They could not have gotten in here, even if they had killed me."

Ermi knew that McEwen was not from his colony. But that was all right. He was a member of the same tribe—the *Lucidi*. "Are you hungry?" he asked.

"Very," said McEwen.

"Then we will eat at once."

McEwen now found himself in a large room. It had several doors that opened out into smaller rooms. Passages led into other chambers and storerooms. It was a home for thousands.

Many tribe members rushed to meet Ermi and McEwen.

"You have had a fight with them?" asked several voices at once.

"Nothing to speak of," said Ermi. "Look after my friend. He just saved my life."

Then the two new friends ate and rested for a while. Later, they got news that the *Sanguineae* had tried an attack on the cave. They were beaten back, though.

"There is war ahead," Ermi finally said to McEwen. "These *Sanguineae* will never let us alone. We will have to fight all of them before we have peace again."

"Good," said McEwen. "I am ready."

"So am I," answered Ermi. "Still it is no light matter. They are our long-time enemy and as powerful as we. If we meet again, you will see real war."

All day there were more reports of attacks by the terrible *Sanguineae*.

At last a meeting was called. The queen came with her chief warriors. There was much loud talking. Finally the *Lucidi* leader called Yumi spoke.

"We must go to war," he said. "The *Sanguineae* will give us no peace. We must get all the tribes of the Shining Slave Makers together. Then we will fight the Red Slave Makers."

Everyone agreed.

Messengers were sent to all parts, calling the huge tribe of Shining Slave Makers to war. After several days, they had all gathered. The big problem now was food. Eventually they hoped to take it from the *Sanguineae*. But for now they had to hunt for it themselves. So that's what they did. They went out and ate every kind of living thing they could find. But still there was not enough.

Both McEwen and Ermi joined in one of these raids. It was a raid upon a colony of *Fuscae*. This colony lived in a nearby forest. The warriors sang as they marched, until they got near the *Fuscae*. Then they became silent.

"Let us not lose track of one another," said McEwen.

"No," agreed Ermi. "But these *Fuscae* are nothing. We will take all they possess without a struggle. See them now? They are already running."

Ermi nodded toward several *Fuscae* who were scurrying off in terror. The *Lucidi* sent up a great shout and chased after them.

McEwen took pleasure in the sport of killing. He tumbled them with rushes of his body. Then he crushed them with his mandibles and poisoned them with his sting.

"Do you need help?" Ermi called out.

"Yes, bring me more of the enemy," joked McEwen.

Soon the deadly work was over. The two comrades gathered a mass of food. Then they joined the returning band, singing as they went.

"Yes! Tomorrow, we will meet the *Sanguineae*," Ermi said. "It is agreed. The leaders are talking about it now."

McEwen was pleased. A strong desire for combat was now upon him.

When they got back to camp, a large number of the tribe was in motion. Thousands upon thousands of them were prepared for action.

"What's the matter?" asked Ermi.

"The *Sanguineae*!" was the answer. "They are returning."

Ermi turned to McEwen. "Take courage," he said. "Now we're in for it."

A huge stir followed. Vast numbers of the *Lucidi* were already heading east. McEwen and Ermi joined a band of marching warriors.

"Order!" shouted a voice in their ears. "Fall in line. We are called!"

The two friends obeyed by instinct. They lined up quickly and soon were moving ahead with others, marching through the tall sword trees. In a little while they reached a huge, smooth, open plain. They saw that the fighting had already begun.

Thousands were here—hundreds of thousands! There was little order among the troops. But none was needed, really. All the fights were between individuals or between small groups.

After a few minutes, McEwen found himself separated from Ermi. Suddenly a red warrior was snapping at his throat. He was almost knocked down. But McEwen fought back. He leaped onto the *Sanguineae* and snapped his jaws into his neck.

"Take that!" he said to the enemy.

But no sooner had McEwen defeated one foe than another one came at him. His enemies were on every side. They were hard, tough fighters like himself and Ermi. One after another they rushed and tore and sawed with amazing force. McEwen faced his new foe swiftly. While the red warrior was going for his head, McEwen grabbed him by the neck. He jabbed his sting into his enemy's throat and shot poison into him. That finished him off.

McEwen looked around. He saw dead warriors everywhere, both friend and foe. Somehow he thought nothing of the terrible sight. It was *wonderful*, he thought, *mysterious*—

One enemy after another came at him. Time after time he fought back. Fighting seemed to come naturally to him. His enemies died one after another—broken, poisoned, sawed in two. McEwen began to count and take joy in the numbers he had killed. It seemed like a dream.

Finally, four of the *Sanguineae* came at him at once. McEwen went down, almost helpless. One seized a leg, another an antenna. A third jumped and sawed at his neck. McEwen did not care. It was all war, and he would fight to the last shred of his strength. Then he seemed to black out. When he opened his eyes again, Ermi was beside him.

"Well?" said Ermi.

"Well?" answered McEwen.

"By the time I reached you, you were about done for."

"Was I?" McEwen answered. "How are things going?"

"I cannot tell yet," said Ermi. "All I know is that you were in bad shape. Two of them were dead, but the other two were about to finish you off."

"You should have left me to them," said McEwen. He could feel the weight of death pushing him down.

"I *am* done for, you know," he said to Ermi. "I cannot live. I felt myself dying some time ago."

He closed his eyes and began to shake. In another moment—

* * *

McEwen opened his eyes. Strangely enough he was looking out across a city park. Men and women were walking by, talking to each other. It was all so strange—so unlike what he had seen so recently. Now he could see tall buildings in the distance. Instead of the sword trees, he saw beech trees and flowers. In wonder, he jumped to his feet. Then he sank back down again. A man walking by gave him a curious look.

"I must have been asleep," he said to himself. "That's it! I've been dreaming. And what a dream!"

McEwen shut his eyes again. For some strange reason, he wished that he was back where he had been in his dream. An odd feeling filled his heart—like missing an old friend.

When McEwen opened his eyes again, memories of his dream began to fade. Still—at his feet lay the battlefield. Or so he thought.

Yes—there—only a few feet away! A

dry area was covered with ants. He stared down at it, searching for the details of a lost world. As he leaned closer, he saw that indeed a giant battle was going on. Dead ants were scattered everywhere! And thousands upon thousands were striking out at each other.

"Why, I was just *there*," McEwen said to himself. He felt dazed. "I died there—or almost did—in my dream."

Stooping closer, he could see the two armies of red ants and black ants clearly. Were the black ones—the Shining Slave Makers—winning?

For a long time McEwen stood there watching, lost in wonder. There were worlds *within* worlds, he thought. But which ones were real—and which were only dreams? Then it came to him that *all* the worlds had feelings, struggle—and sorrow.

And it would go on and on, he thought. It would continue until this strange thing called life had ended.

❦

Thinking About
the Stories

The Lost Phoebe

1. Good writing always has an effect on the reader. How did you feel when you finished reading this story? Were you surprised, horrified, amused, sad, touched, or inspired? What elements in the story made you feel that way?

2. Interesting story plots often have unexpected twists and turns. What surprises did you find in this story?

The Cruise of the *Idlewild*

1. The *Idlewild* was only a make-believe ship. Why did the narrator and John turn their ship into a pretend vessel? Do they really believe they are working on a ship? Explain your thinking.

2. Who is the main character in this story? Who are one or two of the minor characters? Describe each of these characters in one or two sentences.

McEwen of the Shining Slave Makers

1. Where does this story take place? Is there anything unusual about it? What effect does the place have on the characters?

2. Often a character's beliefs or feelings are shown through his actions. How does McEwen act toward the ants at the beginning of the story? How does he regard the ants by the end of the story?